espresso
education

Kim's Treehouse
Pirate

Diane Marwood

W
FRANKLIN WATTS
LONDON•SYDNEY

A fantasy story

First published in 2011 by
Franklin Watts
338 Euston Road
London NW1 3BH

Franklin Watts Australia
Level 17/207 Kent Street
Sydney NSW 2000

The Espresso characters are originated and
designed by Claire Underwood and Pesky Ltd.

The Espresso characters are the property of
Espresso Education Ltd.

A CIP catalogue record for this book is
available from the British Library.

ISBN: 978 1 4451 0404 1 (hbk)
ISBN: 978 1 4451 0412 6 (pbk)

Illustrations by Artful Doodlers Ltd.
Art Director: Jonathan Hair
Series Editor: Jackie Hamley
Series Designer: Matthew Lilly

Printed in China

Franklin Watts is a division of
Hachette Children's Books,
an Hachette UK company
www.hachette.co.uk

Kim and Sal were in Kim's treehouse, reading about pirates.

Suddenly, a head poked
through the branches.
It had a beard like a nest
and a black eye patch.

"It's a pirate!" cried Kim.
"I've lost my ship. Have you
seen it?" asked the pirate.
"No, sorry," said Sal.

"I must find a ship,"
said the pirate sadly.
"A tree is no place
for me!"
Sal and Kim felt
sorry for him.

"Let's help him," whispered Kim.
"How?" asked Sal.
"Can you paint a ship?"
asked Kim.
"Yes!" grinned Sal.

"Here's one," said Kim.
Sal started painting.
"That's brilliant!" smiled Kim.
"I hope he likes it!" said Sal.

Sal and Kim held up
the painting.
"Ship ahoy!" cheered
the pirate.

The pirate jumped
into the painting.
"Come on,"
he shouted.

Sal and Kim jumped in.
Salty waves splashed
their faces. Seagulls
screeched above them.

"This is just like my old ship,"
said the pirate. "Where was it?"
"In a book!" laughed Sal.

21

"And here is my treasure
island," smiled the pirate.
Sal and Kim helped the
pirate to dig up his treasure.

Sal, Kim and the pirate
loaded the treasure onto
the ship and sailed away.

"It's time for us to go home,"
said Kim.

Sal painted another picture.

Then Kim and Sal jumped back into the treehouse.
"Goodbye, pirate!" they cried.

Puzzles

Which speech bubbles
belong to the pirate?

Which words describe the pirate
at the start of the story and which
describe him at the end?

miserable

delighted

overjoyed

unhappy

upset

thrilled

An  **swers**

The pirate's speech bubbles are: 1, 3

At the start of the story, the pirate is: miserable, unhappy, upset.

At the end of the story, the pirate is: delighted, overjoyed, thrilled.

Espresso Connections

This book may be used in conjunction with the Literacy area on Espresso to encourage children's own creative speaking and writing. Here are some suggestions.

Become a Pirate

Visit the Pirates resource box in English 2, and then open the Activity arcade. Choose the activity "Design a pirate character".

Ask children to select items to design two pirates, including adding sound.

Look at the pirate words together. Choose some pirate words and drag them onto the picture of the two pirates. You could put in some more pirate words of your own.

Divide the class into two. One side will play the part of one pirate, and one side will play the other.

Let children take turns to act out the parts of the pirates. Start them off with the pirate voice recordings to really get them into the pirate spirit.

Children must try to use one of the pirate words in the sentence they say. This word can then be deleted from the picture.

Write your own story

Visit the "Writing resource box" in English 1, and go to the Activity arcade. Choose the "Writing frame" activity and select "Story – adventure" on the left. Tab through the information that is given about this genre.

Decide together on the opening of your class pirate story, then on the problem(s), the events and the ending.

Then perfect your class story in the writing frame, using the word bank on the left to edit and improve it. Try to use as many pirate words as you can!

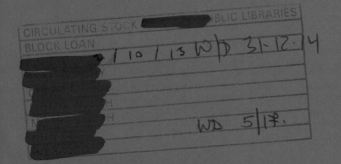